9-1

5/01

School Day
Adventure

For my sister, Debbie—P. H.

To Eric—K. M.

LITTLE SIMON
An imprint of Simon & Schuster Children's Publishing Division
1230 Avenue of the Americas
New York, New York 10020
Text and illustrations copyright © 2000 by Simon & Schuster, Inc.
The names and depictions of Raggedy Ann and Raggedy Andy are trademarks of Simon & Schuster
Manufactured in the United States of America
First Edition
2 4 6 8 10 9 7 5 3 1
Library of Congress Cataloging-in-Publication Data
Hall, Patricia, 1948-
School day adventure / by Patricia Hall ; illustrated by Kathryn Mitter.
p. cm. — (Classic Raggedy Ann & Andy) (Ready-to-read)
Summary: When Marcella takes Raggedy Ann and Andy to school for show-and-tell, they meet som
other interesting characters, including Mac the truck and Petunia the guinea pig.
ISBN 0-689-83247-8
[1. Schools—Fiction. 2. Dolls—Fiction. 3. Toys—Fiction. 4. Show-and-tell presentations—Fiction.]
I. Mitter, Kathy, ill. II. Title. III. Series. IV. Series: Ready-to-read
PZ7.H147515 Sf 2000
[E]-dc21   99-056168

Classic Raggedy Ann & Andy

School Day Adventure

by Patricia Hall
illustrated by Kathryn Mitter

Ready-to-Read

Little Simon

New York   London   Toronto   Sydney   Singapore

It was show-and-tell day at school. All the children had special things to share. Marcella had brought her Raggedy Ann and Andy dolls.

Debbie shared first. "This is Petunia, my real live guinea pig," said Debbie. "She eats lettuce and chews on hay. And sometimes at night she goes 'squeak squeak.'"

"This is my new truck," said Marty. "His name is Mac. He says 'vroom vroom,' and he can go and can carry things. But only if I help."

Then it was Marcella's turn.

"These are my rag dolls, Raggedy Ann and Raggedy Andy," she said. "They aren't alive. And they can't eat or carry things. But Raggedy Andy

can put his feet all the way over his shoulders. And
Raggedy Ann has a real candy heart that says 'I
Love You.'"

"Wonderful show-and-tell, boys and girls!" said Ms. Kelly. "Now, put away your things, and let's put on our alphabet thinking caps.

"Yesterday we learned about the letter 'J.' Who knows what comes next?"

"K!" said Josie.

"Right!" said Ms. Kelly. "And what begins with K?"

"Kitten!" said Pablo.

"Kite!" said David.

"Kelly!" said Marcella. "Ms. Kelly!"

"Right again!" said Ms. Kelly. "Your thinking caps are really working! Now let's get ready for lunch."

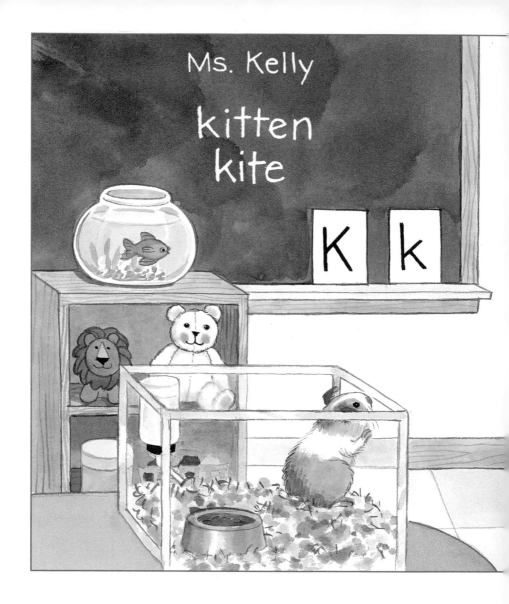

After the children had gone to the cafeteria, the classroom became very, very quiet.

But then there was a rustle inside Marcella's cubb

"Hey," said Raggedy Ann, stretching her rag-doll arms.

"Hey, yourself," said Raggedy Andy, uncurling his
rag-doll legs.

"Hay's for horses—and sometimes me!" said a
squeaky voice from across the room. It was Debbie's
guinea pig, Petunia.

"I didn't know guinea pigs could talk!" said
Raggedy Ann.

"Of course we can," squeaked Petunia. "But I
didn't know rag dolls could walk!"

"You bet we can!" answered Raggedy Andy. "But nly when human beans aren't around."

"He means human beings," explained Raggedy nn.

"Do you really like lettuce and hay like Debbie said?" Raggedy Ann asked.

"As long as I get lots of water to drink," answere Petunia. "Hay makes me thirsty."

"Oh!" laughed Raggedy Ann. "I could never drin water. My candy heart would melt completely away

Just then the Raggedys heard a gulp and a splash "Hello-o-o!" came a bubbly voice. "I'm Gill."

"Hi there!" said the soft voice of the teddy bear. "My name is Teddy, and this is Leo. We love having visitors in Ms. Kelly's classroom."

"Nice to meet you!" said the Raggedys and Petunia at the same time.

"What is a classroom, anyway?" asked
Raggedy Andy. "Is it like Marcella's playroom?"
"Not exactly," said Raggedy Ann gently. "A

assroom is where we are now—where everyone
ears a thinking cap."

Raggedy Andy reached up. Was this his thinking
ap?

Just then there was a *vroom vroom* and a *honk honk*. Out of Marty's cubby rolled Mac the truck.

"Greetings!" he said.

"Wow!" said Raggedy Andy. "I thought you couldn't go unless Marty helped you."

"Oh, yeah?" said Mac. "Hop in!"

"Leaving so soon?" gulped Gill.

"Watch out for the table leg!" warned Teddy.

"Have a great time!" squeaked Petunia.

"Hang on!" cried Mac. "We're rolling now!"

"This is fun!" laughed Raggedy Ann. She loved ride in the car.

"Phew!" said Raggedy Andy. "That was a close one!"

"Mac! Watch out!" cried out Raggedy Andy.

Raggedy Ann stepped on the brakes. Mac rolled to a stop.

"Wow!" said Mac. "Close call! Maybe we should be getting back."

"You're right," said Raggedy Ann after a moment. "But how? All the doors look alike."

"Gosh," said Raggedy Andy. "Look at all of them. I wish I knew how to read."

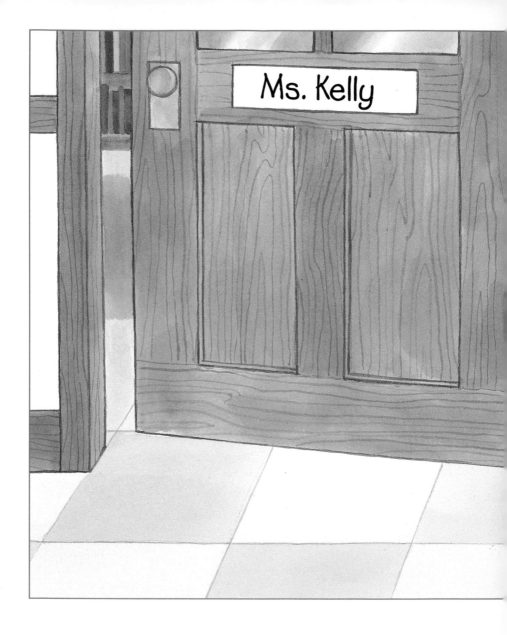

Then Raggedy Andy remembered his thinking ca
As soon as he put it on, he felt smarter. "Look!" he
cried. "The letter 'K'!"

"The one for kitten and kite?" asked Raggedy An

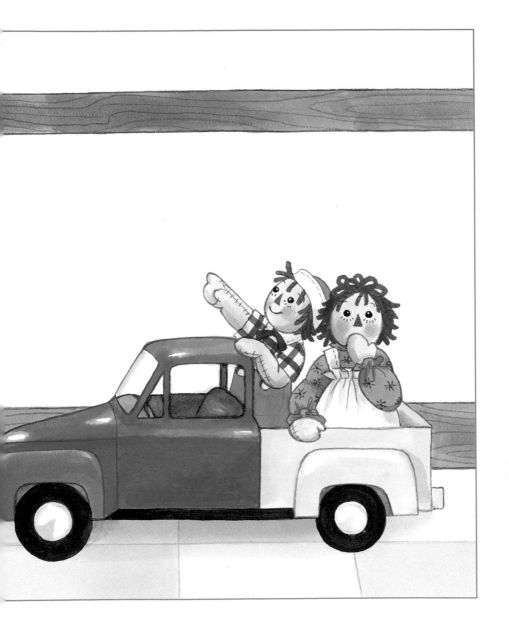

"Yes!" said Raggedy Andy. "And Kelly! Ms. Kelly starts with the letter 'K'!"

Now Mac and the Raggedys knew just where to go.

"They're back!" squeaked Petunia.

"Finally," gulped Gill.

"Are we glad to see you!" said Teddy and Leo together.

"Quick!" said Mac. "I hear the children!"

The class came in that very minute.

"We just made it!" whispered Raggedy Ann.

Later that night at home, Marcella gave the Raggedys an extra-special good night hug. "I wa proud of you at show-and-tell today," she said.

The Raggedys didn't say a word. They waited quietly until all the lights were out and Marcella had gone to bed.

Then Raggedy Ann and Andy told the other
dolls all about their exciting day at school.

"Weren't you scared?" asked the Camel with
the Wrinkled Knees, when he heard about the
Raggedys' ride with Mac.

"Oh, no," said Raggedy Andy. "We had a lot of fun!"

"I'll bet it was fun!" said Uncle Clem. He loved adventure.

"It was until we got lost," said Raggedy Ann.

"How did you find your way back?" asked the Camel with the Wrinkled Knees.

"Easy," grinned Raggedy Andy. "I just put on m thinking cap!"

And with that, the dolls said good night and fe asleep with their shoe-button eyes wide open, the way rag dolls always do.